PRAYING FOR YOUR
WIFE
A SIX-WEEK PRAYER GUIDE
FOR CHRISTIAN MEN

Billy Taylor

Worshiphouse Publishing
FORT WORTH, TEXAS

Billy Taylor/Worshiphouse Inc
PO Box 820505, Ft Worth, TX 76182
www.worshiphouse.com

Publisher's Note: Although this is a work of nonfiction, names, characters, places, and incidents have been changed. Any resemblance to actual people, living or dead, or to businesses, companies, events, institutions, or locales is completely coincidental.

Unless otherwise indicated, Scripture quotations are taken from the New American Standard Bible © The Lockman Foundation 1960, 1962, 1963, 1968, 1971, 1972, 1973, 1975, 1977, 1995. Used by Permission.

Scripture quotations marked as,

NIV are taken from the Holy Bible, New International Version, NIV © 1973, 1978, 1984, 2001 by Biblica, Inc. Used by permission of Zondervan. All rights reserved worldwide.

ESV are taken from the English Standard Bible © 2001 by Crossway Bibles, a division of Good News Publishers.

NLT are taken from Holy Bible, New Living Translation. © 1996, 2004, 2007. Used by permission Tyndale House Publishers, Inc. Wheaton, Illinois 60189. All rights reserved.

HCSB are taken from the Holman Christian Standard Bible, © 1999, 2000, 2002, 2003, by Holman Bible Publishers. Used by permission

Cover Photo: João Silas

Praying for Your Wife/ Billy Taylor -- 1st ed. b
ISBN 978-1-7322727-0-5

Dedication

To my friend Fray Webster, your support and encouragement helped me step out and trust God. You are a true Barnabas.

Contents

Introduction

This might be one of the most important books you have picked up in a long time. Learning to pray for your wife will transform your marriage and your personal prayer life. Few things are as important as you learning to pray effectively for your wife.

This won't be a long introduction for a couple of reasons. First, men like short books, so I am not going to take up a lot of space telling you why you need to pray for your wife. Second, the real power of this book is in you actually praying for your wife, not in me explaining how important it is. However, I do want to give you some background on how this book came to be.

A few years ago, my wife and I were going through an especially difficult time. We weren't considering divorce, but murder was definitely on the table. Even though we had been married for many years, we had grown apart. We were living two separate lives under the same roof. Her focus was on our kids, and I was deeply involved in ministry.

Over time, we worked through our issues, and as we came out of this difficult time, I realized what a terrible job I had done praying for my wife. I was a pastor. I was preaching, leading discipleship programs, and counseling people in the church. I was helping everyone in the church but was spiritually neglecting the most important person in my life.

The more I thought about this and spoke with other men, the more I realized I wasn't alone. Christian husbands are failing to pray for their wives faithfully and effectively. If I, as a pastor, was struggling with praying for my wife, I figured it must be even more difficult for other Christian men.

Certainly, we all have good intentions. How many times have you raised your hand in a church service, at a retreat, or conference, and committed to pray for your wife? But soon, you forget that commitment, get distracted, and feel like a failure.

We fail to effectively pray for our wives for at least three reasons. First, most of us struggle with our own prayer lives. We know that we should be good at prayer, but most of us aren't. We might never admit it at church, but most of our prayer lives are weak and ineffective.

Another reason we fail at praying for our wives is that we don't know what to pray for at all. Once we get past, "God help her be a good mom and wife," we typically run out of gas. We wind up praying the same thing over and over, feeling like we are just wasting our time.

Finally, we neglect to pray for our wives because we don't have a plan. We may be great at projecting out next quarter's sales figures or planning the details of our next project, but when it comes to how to pray for our wives, we don't know where to start.

I wrote *Praying for Your Wife* with the goal of helping you develop a consistent and effective prayer life that enriches your life, your wife's life, your family's lives, and your marriage. This book will give you everything you need to become consistent and effective in praying for your wife over the course of six weeks.

First and foremost, this book is going to show you what to pray for. It will give you 42 topics and scriptures to pray over. By the end of these 42 days, you will have a resource of prayer topics you can draw from to pray for your wife.

Each day includes a sample prayer. If prayer is new to you, you can just pray the sample prayer. If you are more mature in your prayer life, it can be the starting point for praying for your wife in more personalized ways.

I am excited to see what God does in your life and in your marriage as you begin praying daily for your wife. Learning to pray for your wife is going to transform you, your wife, and your marriage.

As you begin praying for your wife, God is going to get into the middle of your marriage, and when God gets involved, great things begin to happen.

Getting Started

As with any new venture, how you start has a lot to do with your success. I want you to be successful in developing a new habit of praying for your wife. So many men struggle with being the spiritual leader of their families. By praying for your wife every day, you are taking the first step toward becoming the spiritual leader you want to be.

As you begin praying for your wife every day and deepening the scope of these prayers, some exciting things are going to happen in your marriage. First, your prayer life will improve. So many of us have a hard time spending consistent time in prayer. By praying for your wife daily, the quantity and quality of your prayer time will improve. As the old saying says, "She needs the prayer, and you need the practice."

As you pray daily for your wife, she will see your commitment as an act of love. She will experience a new level of love and care from you. As she sees you praying for her, she will develop a new confidence in the Lord and in your love for her. As you pray for her, she will feel loved.

Next, when you pray for your wife, you are drawn closer together. When your wife realizes you are serious about praying for her, she will mention things you can pray for her. This will open new levels of intimacy. You will find yourselves talking about struggles and issues you have never discussed before. You will also find God doing a new work in both of your lives.

Finally, when you begin praying for your wife, God shows up in your marriage. When God shows up, good things happen. As you pray for your wife, you are inviting God to work in her life and yours as never before. He will strengthen your marriage as you call out to Him for your wife.

You are not alone. Thousands of men from across the country and over 97 countries have gone through the online version of *Praying for Your Wife*. Having taught thousands of men to pray for their wives, I have learned a few things about how to build the habit of praying for your wife.

Here are six ways you can get off to a great start and ensure that your habit sticks:

Make a Commitment and Go Public

Don't just read through this book. Commit to building a habit of praying for your wife. This may be the most important decision you make this year. As you build a habit of praying for your wife daily, you will see transformation in her life, your life, and your marriage.

As step one, make your commitment, then go public about it. There is something about going public that creates accountability. Tell other guys you know, share it on social media, and especially share it with your wife. Tell your her you are committing to pray for her for the next 42 days. By telling her, you are raising the stakes of your commitment. You can even ask her to pray for you to be faithful and committed to building this new habit of prayer.

Find a Friend or Start a Group

Going it alone is always harder. I have found that men who go through *Praying for Your Wife* together, are often more successful than those who go it alone. So, invite a friend to go through *Praying for Your Wife* with you. If you are part of a small group or Sunday school, you can invite the guys in your group to go through the *Praying for Your Wife* with you.

I have created a discussion guide you can download free of charge at www.prayingforher.com .

Set a Time, Set a Place

Make praying for your wife a part of your morning ritual. Most of us would never leave for work without brushing our teeth (at least I hope not). If you are like me, you never forget to brush your teeth, too.

Brushing my teeth is part of my morning ritual; it's the first thing I do after I take a shower. Make praying for your wife a part of your morning ritual. Set a time and place where you can stop and pray for your wife every morning.

The first thing most of us check in the morning is our phone. Why not place this book near your phone and start the day by praying for your wife?

Use the Sample Prayers

In each prayer day, there is a sample prayer. If you are new to prayer, you can simply pray the prayer as it is written. However, it's much better to use the sample prayer as the starting point. Let the sample prayer be the jumping-off point for your own prayer. That way, you can personalize it for your wife and what's going on in your life together. Remember, the purpose is to pray, so don't just go through the motions.

Use the Copy and Paste Feature

At the end of each prayer day, you will find a section called "Text Message." When you complete each prayer, take a moment and text or email this message to your wife. This simple tool will encourage her and let her know what you are praying for her that day. You will be amazed at how many times what you are praying for her is exactly what she needs for that day.

Allow God to Speak to You

As you read through the daily prayer guide, don't be surprised if God speaks to you about your own life. Men often tell me that God speaks to them as they prepare to pray for their wives. If, for example, their daily topic is for their wife to have more patience, guys hear God speaking to them about their need for patience.

As you pray for your wife, allow God to speak to your own heart. It may amaze at how one day's topic will not only be helpful for your wife but for you as well.

When You Miss a Day

No one is perfect, and there will be times when you miss a day or two. It's okay, don't worry about it. Focus on the long game. You are building a habit, not going through a program. If you miss a day, just pick up where you left off. Don't try to catch up, just start again. There is no need to beat yourself up or feel guilty.

Starting a new habit is going to take some time. You are going to miss a few days here and there. Building a new habit takes some time, so keep going and don't give up.

Encourage Your Wife to Pray for You

Because you are committing to pray for your wife, why not encourage her to pray for you, too? There is a companion version of this program that can help your wife learn how to pray for you.

For more information, go to **www.prayingforhim.com.**

I Am Praying for You

Learning to pray for your wife can be one of the most important habits you build into your marriage. My prayer is that this book will be the launching point in praying for your wife.

I believe that as you pray for your wife, God will do some amazing things in your wife's life, your life, and in your marriage. I believe God calls every Christian husband to pray for his wife daily. I am praying God does a wonderful work in your life, your wife's life, and in your marriage. I am praying this is the beginning of a life-long habit of praying for your wife.

I'd love to hear how God works in your marriage. Pease drop me a note at billy@worshiphouse.com and tell me your story.

Now, it's time to start praying for your wife.

DAY 1

She is God's Gift to Me

Fathers can give their sons an inheritance of houses and wealth, but only the LORD can give an understanding wife.

Proverbs 19:14 (NLT)

Your wife is a gift from God. Your parents can pass down many things, but only God can give you a thoughtful wife. It's the hand of God that matches a man to a woman. Money, land, and wealth are all fleeting, but there is something special about growing old with a woman. An understanding wife is a highly capable woman. She is an asset, not a liability to her husband. If you have a good wife, she is a gift from the Lord.

If you are struggling in your marriage, it's more important than ever to pray for your wife. As you come to God and allow Him to work in your marriage, you will find He can take the mistakes and struggles you have gone through and turn them into His gift to you.

Do you see your wife as a gift from God? Do you treat your wife as a gift from God? Your wife needs to know that you cherish and treasure her. So, as you pray for her today, pray you will also express just how precious she is to you.

Sample Prayer

Father, thank You for giving (*insert wife's name*) to me. Thank You that she is a precious gift from You. Help me to treasure her and never take her for granted. Help me to express just what a gift she is to me. Thank You for bringing us together. Help us grow closer to each other as we grow closer to You.

In Jesus' name, amen.

Text Message

(*Insert wife's name*), you are God's special gift to me. Today, I am thanking God He brought you to me. Together, we are a match made in heaven. There is nothing that would make me happier than to spend the rest of my life with you.

DAY 2
Fill Her With Joy

Now may the God of hope fill you with joy and peace as you believe in Him, so that you may overflow with hope by the power of the Holy Spirit.

Romans 15:13 (HCSB)

In a world of anxiety, stress, and depression, God's Word gives us joy. Joy is a central theme in the Christian life. It is the second fruit of the Spirit and the celebration of our life in Christ.

Of course, it doesn't mean that everything will always be perfect, and it is no guarantee of a problem-free life. However, joy is the confident expression that God is in control. Joy has more to do with your inner heart than your outer circumstances.

The source of joy is not your situation but your relationship with God. Throughout the Book of Psalms, David declares there is abundant joy in the presence of God. Joy is the overflowing attitude of a person walking in fellowship with the Lord Jesus. When you walk in God's presence, you experience joy.

As you pray for your wife, pray that joy and peace become the natural expressions of her life. Pray the Lord fills her with the Holy Spirit's power so that hope fills her life. Agree with the Apostle Paul by praying that her life overflows with joy and peace as she puts her trust in Christ.

Sample Prayer

Father, today I pray You will fill (*insert wife's name*) with Your joy and peace. I pray she walks in Your presence today and experiences the abundant joy of being filled with the Holy Spirit. I pray she will not look at her circumstances but will seek Your face, knowing You are in control of her life. Fill her with joy and peace today.
In Jesus' name, amen.

Text Message

(*Insert wife's name*), today I am praying God fills you with His joy and peace. I am praying you won't focus on your circumstances, but on the God who loves you. I am praying for hope, peace, and to joy fill your heart today.

DAY 3
God is Her Refuge

This I declare about the Lord: He alone is my refuge,
my place of safety; he is my God, and I trust him.

Psalm 91:2 (NLT)

We all have times when we feel we are under attack. It may seem like everyone is against us. Fear and insecurity creep into our souls, and we need a secure place of protection and safety.

Every day, your wife is under attack. Our culture and the forces of darkness mount a constant barrage against her. There is only one place she can take refuge in the middle of the battle, and that is in the Lord. The Psalmist declares that his only refuge, his only safe place, is in the Lord. He will put his faith and trust in Him.

Today, your wife needs security and protection in the heat of the battle. She must find her safe refuge amid the strife and turmoil in the Lord. He is her protection and there is no need to fear.

Let's ask the Father to remind her that the doors of God's protection are always open. All she needs to do is run to Him.

Sample Prayer

Father, I pray You will remind *(insert wife's name)* today that You are her security and protection. I pray as she faces the stresses and attacks today, she will turn to You as her refuge. Protect her and keep her safe in Your arms. Remind her to put her faith and trust in You, for You alone can be the place of safety she needs.

In Jesus' name, amen.

Text Message

(Insert wife's name), today, the Lord Jesus is your safety and protection. When stresses and trials come against you, run to the only one who can truly be trusted. He is your refuge and strength. Trust in Him.

DAY 4
Her Sins Are Forgiven

For He rescued us from the domain of darkness and transferred us to the kingdom of His beloved Son, in whom we have redemption, the forgiveness of sins.

Colossians 1:13-14

Although we know Christ has forgiven our sins, it is easy to hold onto the guilt and pain of our sins. So many Christians claim forgiveness but still carry the burdens of their sins on their shoulders. They don't expect to live in victory over sin, and they feel guilty every time they come before God in prayer.

The Psalmist describes the forgiven person as "blessed" (Ps 32:1). Blessed means "happy." Joy and happiness are the hallmarks of those who are forgiven. One of the meanings of the word "forgiven" is "to send away, never to be seen again." In forgiving us, God sends our sins away. When God forgives our sin, He never brings it back again.

When we realize our sins have been "sent away," we experience new freedom and joy in our lives. As you pray for your wife today, pray she remembers that her sins have been forgiven. She doesn't have to carry her sin; Jesus paid for it on the cross. Pray the joy of the Lord is released in her as she remembers her sin has been "sent away."

Sample Prayer

Father, I pray that today, (*insert wife's name*) will remember that her sin has been forgiven and removed. I pray she feels a new sense of freedom and joy as she recalls that You have sent her sins away. Help her forget her failures and press on to know You.

In Jesus' name, amen.

Text Message

(*Insert wife's name*), Jesus has forgiven your sins. You don't have to carry the guilt or pain of your sin any longer. Christ has sent your sin away, never to be seen again. Today, I pray you sense the freedom and joy of being forgiven.

DAY 5
A Woman of Courage

Be strong and courageous, do not be afraid or tremble at them, for the Lord your God is the one who goes with you. He will not fail you or forsake you.

Deuteronomy 31:6

When Joshua became leader of the Children of Israel, it was a daunting promotion. Moses had led the Children of God through the wilderness, and now Joshua was stepping into the shoes of the most respected leader in history. Imagine the fear and insecurity Joshua must have felt! How do you follow the man who freed God's people from the slavery of Egypt, parted the Red Sea, and fed the people with manna?

Sometimes, we face challenges and problems that make us want to run and hide. We may feel insecure or inadequate. But we can be courageous because we know what Joshua knew; it is not about my strength, but God's strength in me. It is not the person but the God behind the person that makes the difference.

As you pray for your wife today, pray that she walks with courage. Pray she remembers that her courage comes from knowing that God is with her and will never forsake her. There is no need to fear when the God of the universe is on her side. She can be courageous not because of her strength but because God is fighting the battles for her.

Sample Prayer

Father, be with (*insert wife's name*) and give her courage. Remind her that You are with her and that You fight the battles for her. Let her fear be overcome by knowing that You are with her, and You will never fail or forsake her. In Jesus' name, amen.

Text Message

(*Insert wife's name*), today, I am praying that you walk in the courage of the Lord. I am asking God to strengthen you and remind you that He fights the battles for you. As you take on tasks and problems that you might be fearful of accepting, remember that God is with you, and He will never leave you stranded.

DAY 6
A Heart of Compassion

She extends her hand to the poor, and she stretches out her hands to the needy.

Proverbs 31:20

Compassion is a missing quality in our world today. It is so easy to get caught up in our little world and forget about the poor and needy around us. We see the hurting and quickly turn our heads. We think it's someone else's responsibility. We think the government should be doing something, but throughout scripture, we see the church not only meeting the spiritual needs of the disenfranchised but also their physical needs. A compassionate person sees a need and does whatever they can to help.

Generosity means living with an understanding that what you have is not your own. It is being mindful that I am just a conduit for the resources of God. Because I am not the source, I can give what I have to help others. The

Proverbs 31 woman is not so caught up in her world that she misses the needs of those around her. She is ready and willing to help anyone in need. She doesn't give out of guilt because she genuinely wants to help.

Today, as you pray for your wife, pray God gives her a heart of compassion. Pray she opens her heart and her hands to those in need. Ask God to open her eyes to the needs around her.

Sample Prayer

Father, today I pray You will give (*insert wife's name*) a heart of compassion. I pray she will open her heart and hands to help anyone she sees in need. I pray she will not turn her head away from the needy but will reach out and help in any way she can.

Text Message

(*Insert wife's name*), today I was reminded of how much we need compassion. It is easy to overlook those in need and simply focus on ourselves. I am praying you will have a special opportunity to meet a need in someone's life today. I am praying that compassion fills your heart today. life today.

DAY 7
What God Began, He Will Finish

For I am confident of this very thing, that He who began a good work in you will perfect it until the day of Christ Jesus.

Philippians 1:6

God is always working on our behalf. We might not always see it, and we might not always feel it, but God is at work. God began his work when we came to Christ and will complete His work when we see Jesus face-to-face.

Because we know God is working for us, we should strive to have greater confidence and joy. God will not give up on us. He is like the potter who reshapes the clay into the image he desires. God is molding and shaping us into the image of Christ. Even though we are unfaithful, the God we serve is faithful to complete His plan for us.

God is working in your wife to complete His plan for her. He created her with a special purpose in mind and is working to achieve that purpose. As she allows, God will work through her to complete His good work.

As you pray for your wife today, pray she remembers what God began in her, He will complete. Pray she remembers God is at work even when she doesn't feel it or see it.

Sample Prayer

Father, I pray You will remind (*insert wife's name*) that what You began in her, You will complete. I pray when she is discouraged, she remembers You are working in her to make her like Christ. Help her to allow You to mold and use her as You desire.

In Jesus' name, amen.

Text Message

(*Insert wife's name*), today, God is working on your behalf. What He began in you, He will complete. I am praying that even when you can't see it, you will remember God is working to bring about His perfect plan in your life. I pray that knowing God is working in you will give you will give you new joy and confidence.

DAY 8
Peace with Her Past

Brethren, I do not regard myself as having laid hold of it yet; but one thing I do: forgetting what lies behind and reaching forward to what lies ahead, I press on toward the goal for the prize of the upward call of God in Christ Jesus.

Philippians 3:13–14

We all have a past. We all carry emotional baggage from past mistakes, failures, accusations, and hurt. Words spoken to us as a child can still sting after many, many years. The good news is that Christ has set us free from the past. He forgave our sins and made us new creatures in Him.

If there was ever anyone who had baggage from the past, it was the Apostle Paul. How many Christians had been persecuted, imprisoned, and killed because of him? Yet, Paul allowed Christ to bring peace to his past. Paul said he had to forget everything in the past so he could pursue Christ more fully.

As you pray for your wife today, pray she forgets her past mistakes and sin. Pray she realizes her past has been forgiven by the blood of Christ. No matter what she has gone through, Christ has redeemed, restored, and made her one of His precious children.

Sample Prayer

Father, help (*insert wife's name*) see her past mistakes as forgiven and her hurts and pains as healed by the broken body of Christ on the cross. Help her set her eyes on You and not look back. May she see herself as Your precious child. Remind her today that the old things have passed away and that she is a new creature in You.
In Jesus' name, amen.

Text Message

(*Insert wife's name*), today, I am praying that you remember that the past is the past. There is nothing you can do about it and nothing you can do to change it. Christ took your past to the cross. He forgave your sin and healed your hurt. Today, set your eyes on Jesus and forget what is behind you.

Take up the Full Armor of God

Therefore, take up the full armor of God, so that you will be able to resist in the evil day, and having done everything, to stand firm.

Ephesians 6:13

Although we can't see it, we wake up every morning on a battlefield. There are forces bent on our destruction. Satan and his dark forces have your wife in their sights. The Bible says Satan roars like a lion, looking for who he can destroy. The Book of Revelation calls him the "great deceiver." Today, Satan has made a custom plan for your wife's destruction.

The good news is that God has given her spiritual armor with the power to not only stand against Satan's attack but to live in victory over him. However, she must put on that armor every day to be victorious.

If you knew your wife was going off to war today, you would pray for her safety, protection, and victory. She is going off to war. Pray she puts on the full armor of God and trusts in His strength and might. Pray she stays close to the Father and stands firmly against the attacks of Satan. Pray that she puts on the full armor of God and resists the attack of Satan.

Sample Prayer

Father, keep (insert wife's name) close to You today. Remind her that she is in a spiritual battle every moment of the day. Help her put on her spiritual armor. Help her listen for Your word today. Protect her from the lies Satan will whisper in her ear. Strengthen her with Your might and power. Today, I claim spiritual victory for my wife.

In Jesus' name, amen.

Test Message

(*Insert wife's name*), today, you will be in a spiritual battle. Satan is going to try and deceive you. Put on the spiritual armor God has given you. I am praying for Your protection and strength to stand against Satan's attacks.

DAY 10
Cast Her Cares on You

Casting all your care on Him, because He cares about you.

1 Peter 5:7 (HSBC)

We all carry anxieties, worries, and fears. Carrying these burdens creates a tremendous amount of stress in our lives. The pressures and concerns of life can often feel like a thousand-pound weight on our shoulders. But we have a choice. We can either carry our anxieties ourselves or place them on Christ.

Your wife lives in a stressful world, but God invites her to place her worry, fears, and anxieties onto Him. Every fear and worry is an invitation to pray. She has someone who will take away her worries, cares, and fears. She can confidently place her burdens and worries on Christ because He cares for her. God is not ignorant of her situation. He knows the details of her life and cares about them. He is ready to accept all the burdens she places on Him.

Today, your wife may feel the world's weight on her shoulders. She may be filled with worry and anxiety. As you pray for her, pray she places those worries and cares on Christ's shoulders. He is willing and more than able to carry them because He cares for her.

Sample Prayer

Father, today, I pray that (insert wife's name) will not carry her fears, worries, and cares but will place them all on You. I pray she will remember just how much You love her and will release all of her anxiety onto You. Give her a new and deeper understanding of how much You love her. Let her walk in Your freedom today as she places all her cares on You.

In Jesus' name, amen.

Text Message

(*Insert wife's name*), today, I am praying you place all your cares, worries, anxieties, and fears onto God. He knows the burdens you carry and offers to carry them for you. I am praying you have a wonderful day as you cast all your cares onto Christ.

DAY 11
You Found a Good Thing

He who finds a wife finds a good thing and obtains favor from the Lord.

Proverbs 18:22

From the beginning of creation, God has blessed marriage. When God placed man in the Garden of Eden, He said it was not good for him to be alone (Genesis 2:18). When you found your wife, you found a good thing.

Notice that God didn't say "perfect" wife. The longer you are married, the easier it is to focus on the imperfections of your wife. It is easy to take her for granted and hold onto past disappointments. No, she's not perfect, but neither are you. However, without her, you would be a lonely man.

If you have ever spent time traveling alone, you know what a blessing your wife is. There are few things lonelier than an empty motel room or an empty house.

Praise God for blessing you with your wife. Forget her flaws and imperfections. Instead, focus on the blessing she is to you. You found a good thing when you found her. Today, remember the good things she has brought into your life. Life is always easier and a lot more fun with someone by your side.

Sample Prayer

Father, thank You for bringing (*insert wife's name*) into my life. When I found her, I found a good thing. Thank You for the friendship, companionship, and love she brings into my life. Today, help me to show my appreciation to her. Help me focus on what a blessing she is instead of focusing on her shortcomings.
In Jesus' name, amen.

Text Message

(*Insert wife's name*), today, I am praising God that He brought you to me. You are such a blessing to my life. Thank you for being my wife, friend, lover, and companion.

DAY 12
Help Her Spend Time with You

In the early morning, while it was still dark, Jesus got up, left the house, and went away to a secluded place and was praying there.

Mark 1:3

We all live busy lives. From the moment we begin our day to the moment our head hits the pillow; we are always on the run. There is no question that Jesus also lived a busy life. He was always teaching, performing miracles, and leading the disciples.

But no matter how busy we are, we must always make time for what is important to us. For example, we all have our morning rituals.

We know that it takes time to shower, get dressed, and brush our teeth. But how often do we include spending time with God as part of our morning ritual? Why is it so easy to remember to brush our teeth but so hard to set time aside to be with God?

Could it be that we have placed brushing our teeth as a higher priority than time with God? To grow in her walk with God, your wife must have a daily time of prayer and Bible study. Sunday morning worship is great, but it can never replace a personal devotion time. Prayer and Bible study are two places where God speaks to her. As you pray for your wife today, pray she develops a personal daily time of worship and prayer. If you know she already has a personal time with God, ask the Lord to give her a wonderful experience with Him today.

Sample Prayer

Father, I pray (*insert wife's name*) will spend time with You every day. I pray she will make it as high a priority as brushing her teeth is. Let her time with You become part of her daily routine. Help her to never face her busy day without spending time with You.
In Jesus' name, amen.

Text Message

(*Insert wife's name*), I am pray that prayer and Bible study become part of your daily morning ritual. I know you are busy, and I am praying you never face a busy day without spending time with God.

DAY 13
Leave a Godly Heritage

*For I am mindful of the sincere faith within you,
which first dwelt in your grandmother Lois and your
mother Eunice, and I am sure that it is in you as
well.*

2 Timothy 1:5

Our children see the good and the bad in our lives. Whether we like it or not, they see how we really live. Many people put on a good show for Sunday morning worship but live a different life in the privacy of their homes.

Faith that lasts from generation to generation must be sincere faith. True faith in Christ is never hypocritical or deceptive. It never puts on a front for others but is filled with honest love for God.

The above verse from 2 Timothy lists three generations of believers: Timothy, his mother Eunice, and his grandmother Lois. What a wonderful comment on the faith of Lois. What a great heritage, to see your faith in Christ passed down to your children and your children's children.

Today, pray your wife lives in such a way that her children will not only see her faith but will pass that faith along to their children. Pray she lives in sincere faith before those who know her best.

Sample Prayer

Father, I pray (*insert wife's name*) lives a life of such sincere faith that our children see her genuine love for You. I pray she will be an example to our children, and they will, in turn, pass that faith down to their children. I pray she leaves a godly heritage of genuine, honest, and sincere faith in You.

In Jesus' name, amen.

Text Message

(*Insert wife's name*), today I am praying your walk with Christ will be an example to our children. I am praying they see your honest and sincere faith and that it challenges them to pass faith down to their children. I am praying that you leave a Godly heritage that lasts for generations.

DAY 14
Fill Her With Wisdom

But if any of you lacks wisdom, let him ask of God, who gives to all generously and without reproach, and it will be given to him.

James 1:5

There is a difference between knowledge and wisdom. The world is full of knowledge. Knowledge has to do with facts and skills; wisdom is about how you live and what you do with that knowledge.

God promises that if we need wisdom, all we have to do is ask. It may seem simple, but few of us take advantage of this promise. All of us need God's wisdom in our daily lives. How many problems could we avoid if we just looked to God for wisdom?

Solomon became king when he was still a young man. God offered to give him anything he requested. Imagine the opportunity! He could have asked for power or for all of his enemies to fall before him. He could have asked for riches, but instead, he asked for wisdom. God honored his request, and because of his wisdom, he became one of the wealthiest kings who ever lived. The secret to his success was wisdom from above.

Your wife needs wisdom, too. From the little decisions to the big ones, she needs the wisdom of God every day. Today, as you pray for your wife, ask God to give her wisdom beyond her years. Ask God to place a hunger in her heart for the wisdom only He provides. As she walks in wisdom, let her experience new levels of blessing and success.

Sample Prayer

Father, I pray You will give (*insert wife's name*) Your wisdom. Give her wisdom beyond her years. I pray she will walk in Your wisdom and not trust her own thinking. You promised that if we lack wisdom, You will give it to us freely. I pray You fill her with Your wisdom today.
In Jesus' name, amen.

Text Message

(*Insert wife's name*), I am praying God fills you with His wisdom today. God promises that if we need wisdom, all we need to do is ask. I know you need God's wisdom to deal with the various issues you face today. Ask God for wisdom, and He will give it to you.

Become a Woman of Prayer

Praying at all times in the Spirit with all prayer and supplication. To that end, keep alert with all perseverance, making supplication for all the saints.

Ephesians 6:18 (ESV)

Prayer is the focal point of the Christian life. Through prayer, we have access to the very throne room of God. Prayer transcends time and space. We can pray for someone on the other side of the world and know God can touch them immediately. We can pray for events years in the future and know that God will not forget our prayers.

Unfortunately, few Christians take advantage of the power of prayer. Research shows the average Christian spends less than five minutes a day in prayer. Is it any wonder we have so little power in our lives today?

God is calling your wife to be a woman of prayer, a woman who makes prayer a central part of her life. We see examples of women who called out to God throughout the Bible. It has been said, "We are most powerful when we are on our knees." The doorway to experiencing the power of God in our lives is a life of prayer.

As you pray for your wife, pray she becomes a woman of prayer. Ask the Lord to give her a renewed passion for entering his presence through prayer. Pray she takes time every day to bring her needs and the needs of those around her to the Lord in prayer.

Sample Prayer

Father, I pray that You help (*insert wife's name*) strengthen her personal prayer life. I ask that You build in her a deep hunger and desire to spend more time in prayer. I pray she will give herself, as never before, to becoming a woman of prayer.

In Jesus' name, amen.

Text Message

(*Insert wife's name*), I am praying God gives you a new and deeper desire to spend more time in prayer. When you pray, you bring the power and presence of God to every situation. I am praying you become a true woman of prayer.

Extra Credit: Why not take a few moments today to pray with your wife?

DAY 16
God Delights in Her

For the LORD, your God, is living among you. He is a mighty savior. He will take delight in you with gladness. With his love, he will calm all your fears. He will rejoice over you with joyful songs.

Zephaniah 3:17 (NLT)

Many Christian women spend their lives feeling like God is mad at them. At best, they think God is disappointed with them. No matter how hard they try, they believe they can never live up to God's expectations. They are always mindful of their failures and sin.

What an incredible contrast this verse is to that kind of thinking! God delights in your wife. He rejoices over her the way a father rejoices over his newborn child. When He thinks of your wife, He breaks out in song. Here are five wonderful truths from this verse you can claim for your wife.

- God is with her.

- He is her mighty savior.
- He delights in her.
- He calms her fear with His love.
- He rejoices over her with singing.

As you pray for your wife today, pray these five truths for her. Pray she remembers that God truly delights in her. She can rest in His love to calm all her fears, for He rejoices over her.

Sample Prayer

Father, today, remind (*insert wife's name*) that You are with her. Let her sense Your presence throughout her day. Let her see You as her mighty savior. Let her remember that You delight in her. I pray You will show her that You sing over her the way a young mother sings over her newborn baby. I pray You will calm all her fears with Your love.

In Jesus' name, amen.

Text Message

(*Insert wife's name*), God delights in you! I am praying that God calms all your fears through His love. As you go through your day, remember that God is proud of You. He loves you more than you can understand, and you are His delight.

DAY 17
She Will Love Others

By this all men will know that you are My disciples,
if you have love for one another.

John 13:35

The greatest indicator of our love for God is our love for others. You can't be a true follower of Christ without having a true love for other people.

Paul says in 1 Corinthians 13, that if we have great wisdom, preach to the world, give away everything we have, even give ourselves to be burned alive for the sake of the gospel, but we don't have love, it is all worthless.

True love can only come from God. Love was a defining characteristic of the early church. As the Holy Spirit fills us, the outward expression is love. We are most like our Father when we express love to others. You can only manifest this kind of love as you allow God to love through you.

As you pray for your wife, pray that God fills her heart with His love. Ask the Lord to fill her with His Holy Spirit, and that love be the overflowing expression of her life. Pray that this supernatural love will so freely flow through her that everyone around her will be drawn to faith in Christ Jesus.

Sample Prayer

Father, I pray You fill (*insert wife's name*) with Your supernatural love. I pray that as You fill her with Your presence, love will naturally flow from her life. I pray that everyone she meets will be drawn to You as they see how she loves. I also pray she will have a special opportunity to share Your love today.

In Jesus' name, amen.

Text Message

(*Insert wife's name*), today, I am praying God so fills you with His Holy Spirit that a supernatural love will overflow from your heart. I am praying God gives you a special opportunity to show love to someone today.

DAY 18
Overcome Anxiety

Do not fear, for I am with you; do not anxiously look about you, for I am your God. I will strengthen you; surely, I will help you. Surely, I will uphold you with My righteous right hand.

Isaiah 41:10

Sometimes, fear and anxiety can come sweeping over us like the wind before a storm. Many times, our wives struggle with anxiety and worry. This verse contains four powerful promises your wife can claim over anxiety, fear, and worry.

1. <u>I am with You.</u> Fear and loneliness often go h~~ in~~ hand. How can she walk in fear if the God of ~~tion~~ is with her?

2. <u>I am your God.</u> She has a personal rela~~ip with~~ Him. He is her God. He has claimed ~~she has~~ claimed Him.

3. <u>I will help you.</u> He is not only her God and with her, but He is also actively working in her life, too. He is helping her. How can she be anxious about tomorrow, knowing the God of the universe is helping her?

4. <u>I will uphold you.</u> In her darkest times, when she feels like quitting and giving up, she can rest assured that God is upholding her. God is undergirding her with His love and strength. She will find a firm foundation in Him.

How can your wife ever be anxious and fearful with these four promises from God? Her God is with her, helping and strengthening her.

As you pray for your wife today, pray that she overcomes her anxiety by remembering that God is helping and strengthening her. Ask the Lord to remind her that He is with her and is strengthening her.

Sample Prayer

Father, I pray You help (*insert wife's name*) overcome her anxiety by remembering these four promises. I pray she sees Your presence with her today. When she becomes fearful or worried, remind her that You are with her, helping and strengthening her.

In Jesus' name, amen.

Text Message

(*Insert wife's name*), today, I am praying that you remember that God is with you any time you experience fear or anxiety. He is helping and upholding you. The God you serve will never leave you but will be there for you when you need Him. Today, your God is working for your good, so why be anxious?

She Will Know Her Riches in Christ

I pray that the eyes of your heart may be enlightened, so that you will know what is the hope of His calling, what are the riches of the glory of His inheritance in the saints, and what is the surpassing greatness of His power toward us who believe.

Ephesians 1:18–19

Once, there was a farmer in west Texas who struggled to feed his family. Life was hard, and keeping the family farm afloat was a constant battle. They lived in fear that the next drought or weak harvest would mean losing everything.

One day, as he was drilling a water well, the unexpected happened. Instead of hitting water, they struck oil! Oh, how things changed for this farmer. Gone were the worries of losing the farm or surviving until the harvest. For years, they had struggled, worried, and lived in fear while sitting on millions of dollars of oil.

So often, we have a "get-by" attitude when it comes to our walk with Christ when God has lavished us with His riches. In the above verse, Paul prays that God would open our eyes to the incredible riches we have in Christ Jesus.

Like the farmer, we have incredible blessings available to us. However, for the most part, we are blind to them. We need our spiritual eyes opened. We are not poor Christians hoping to last until we die or Jesus comes. No, we are the saints of God. We have tremendous riches, power, and hope through Jesus Christ.

Today, pray God opens your wife's eyes are to all her riches in Christ.

Sample Prayer

Father, I pray that (*insert wife's name*) sees her riches in You. Open her eyes to a new vision of all You have done for her. Let her see all You have for her and all You want to do through her.
In Jesus' name, amen.

Text Message

(*Insert wife's name*), today, I am praying that God opens your eyes to a deeper understanding of all He has for you. I am claiming Ephesians 1:18-19 for you today. I pray that the eyes of your heart are enlightened, so you will know all the incredible things God has given you.

She is God's Masterpiece

For we are His workmanship, created in Christ Jesus for good works, which God prepared beforehand so that we would walk in them.

Ephesians 2:10

God is always working in your wife's life to make her more like Jesus. Just as a craftsman refines the details of his sculpture, God is molding and forming her for His glory. Only God knows the final image He is creating. She may look at herself and think she is of little value, but God sees her as His precious masterpiece. She is His handiwork, and as the old saying goes, "God don't make no junk!"

According to *Focus on the Family*, the number-one cause of depression in women is low self-esteem. If your wife bases her self-esteem on what she sees today, she may become discouraged. However, God isn't finished with her. He is making her into His masterpiece for His glory. She self-esteem must be based on what God says about her, not what she sees in the mirror. In God's eyes, she is a fine work of art. God created your wife, and He is not finished with her yet.

As you pray for your wife today, pray she sees herself as God's handiwork. Ask the Father to remind her that she is His masterpiece. Pray she is encouraged as she remembers that God is working in her to make her more like Christ. Her job is to allow God to continue His work in her.

Sample Prayer

Father, today, I thank You that (*insert wife's name*) is Your masterpiece. I pray she will remember that You are working in her to make her just like Jesus. I pray that today, she will be encouraged, knowing that You consider her Your masterpiece.
In Jesus' name, amen.

Text Message

(*Insert wife's name*), God places great value in you, and you are His prized work of art. As you go through your day, remember that God is working in you to make you more like Jesus.

DAY 21
She Will Walk in Contentment

*Not that I am speaking of being in need, for I have
learned in whatever situation I am in to be content.*

Philippians 4:11 (ESV)

Every day, advertisers bombard us with messages that we can never be happy unless we have the latest, greatest, and hottest new products. As believers, we know you can't find true happiness in what we wear, where we live, or what we drive. However, it is easy to get caught up in the desire for material things.

There is nothing wrong with wanting nice things, but it will only lead to frustration and anxiety when it becomes your focus. Learning to be happy with what we have releases tremendous peace. You won't find contentment by changing your attitude. True contentment comes when you surrender your life into the hands of God.

Contentment and peace are closely related. When we understand that God is in control, we can be content and live in peace. Did you notice that today's verse proceeds the famous verse, "I can do all things in Christ?" Once we understand that God is in control, we realize that we can do everything God has called us to do.

Today, pray your wife finds contentment in every situation. Pray she seeks the contentment that only comes from the presence of God. Ask for God's strength to resist the media that you can only find happiness in what you wear, what you drive, or where you live.

Sample Prayer

Father, I pray (*insert wife's name*) finds contentment in You. I pray she walks in peace knowing that You are in charge of her life. I pray she won't get caught up in seeking material things but will seek your blessing over everything else. Remind her of all the blessings you have given Her. Help her to see that You are her provision and peace.

In Jesus' name, amen.

Text Message

(*Insert wife's name*), today, I am praying that you live in the complete contentment of Christ and that you remember the wonderful blessings God has given us. I am praying that His peace will go with you throughout your day, and that you find contentment in Him.

DAY 22
Victory Over Her Fear

For God gave us a spirit not of fear but of power and love and self-control.

2 Timothy 1:7 (ESV)

Psychologists tell us we are born with only two fears: the fear of loud noises and the fear of falling. All other fears are learned. We have literally learned to be fearful. Just because we have fears does not mean we have to be ruled by them.

Every day, your wife faces fear. Is she good enough or pretty enough? Many women have a fear of failing or even getting old. These are just a few of the thousands of concerns that run through her mind. At times, her fears may become so real that they become overwhelming.

Your wife doesn't have to live a life full of fear and defeat. Through Christ, she can do more than just face her fears; she can live in victory over them. She doesn't have to be ruled by her emotions; God has given her a sound mind. When she knows how much God loves her, there is no reason for her to live in fear. God has promised her a life ruled by faith and confidence in Christ.

Ask God to give her renewed faith and confidence in Christ so she can overcome every fear that comes into her life.

Sample Prayer
Father, I pray that (*insert wife's name*) will not allow fear to rule her. Help her walk in the power and self-control You have given her. Remind her that You have freed her from the power of fear. Give her victory over her fears today. In Jesus' name, amen.

Text Message
(*Insert wife's name*), today I am praying that you live in the power of Christ. God has not given you a spirit of fear but of power. His Spirit within you gives you a new level of power and self-control.

DAY 23
She is Wonderfully Made

*For You formed my inward parts; You wove me in my
mother's womb. I will give thanks to You, for I am
fearfully and wonderfully made; wonderful are Your
works, and my soul knows it very well.*

Psalm 139:13–14

Our bodies are truly amazing. From how the brain func-
tions to how our bones are connected, our bodies are
amazing machines. The world would have us believe that
we are simply accidents. That we are result of two DNA
strands coming together. Others say we are nothing
more than the result of a million years of evolution.

However, God's word paints a vastly different picture.
The above verse from Psalm 139 reminds us that God was
at work in our lives long before we were born. Before we
ever opened our eyes to this world, God formed and
shaped us. We are not merely DNA accidents but the result of a God who loves and cares for us.

Many women struggle with insecurity and inferiority. They often judge themselves by the world's standards and forget that they are wonderfully and marvelously created. Your wife can stand confidently, knowing that she is an expression of the ever-loving and creative God. He formed her and made her for His glory.

When we thank God for the way He made us, we begin to see past our weaknesses and to the purpose and plan God has for us. We see how He is the master creator who has formed us, and instead of doubting our worth, we praise Him for his work.

Today, pray your wife remembers that she is the work of a divine creator and not a genetic accident. Pray that she sees herself as the handiwork of a loving, creative God.

Sample Prayer

Father, remind (*insert wife's name*) she is wonderfully made. I pray she sees herself as Your marvelous creation. Give her new security and confidence today because she knows she was created by a loving God who made her in His image, and His works are always best.

In Jesus' name, amen.

Text Message

(*Insert wife's name*), you are wonderfully made by a loving God who cares deeply for you. I thank God that He made you just the way you are. Before you were ever born, He made you and formed you for His glory.

Help Me Carry Her Burden

Carry one another's burdens; in this way, you will fulfill the law of Christ.

Galatians 6:2 (HCSB)

In the survey we sent to 8,500 women, one of the most common concerns was getting everything done. Your wife wears many hats, from taking the kids to an unending number of activities to fixing meals and caring for her husband. The adage, "A woman's work is never done," seems to be as true now as ever.

She may feel like she carries the weight of the world on her shoulders. On top of her home responsibilities, she may work outside of the home, giving her an entirely different set of burdens.

Christ showed us the Father's love by living as a servant. Living a life of service is living a life of Christ. How can you serve your wife today? What is one thing you can do today to ease her burden and lift her load? By helping her with a practical need, you can show her how much you love her.

So today, in addition to praying for your wife, ask God to show you at least one way you can serve your wife by helping her around the house or in any way God directs you.

Sample Prayer

Father, thank You for (*insert wife's name*). I know she does so much for our family and me. I know often I don't recognize all the things she does and the burdens she carries. Open my eyes to how I can show her my love by serving her today. Show me one way I can help her today. In Jesus' name, amen.

(Don't text this to your wife unless you intend to go through with it!)

Text Message

(*Insert wife's name*), I know I can be completely unaware of everything you do for the family and me. Thank you for all you do. Today, I am asking God to open my eyes to how I can help you more.

DAY 25
She Will Abide in You

Abide in Me, and I in you. As the branch cannot bear fruit of itself unless it abides in the vine, so neither can you unless you abide in Me.

John 15:4

Earlier in this chapter of the Bible, Jesus said, "He is the vine, and we are the branches" (v.1). The vine supplies everything the branch needs for life and growth. Jesus said that we would never please God unless we abide in Him.

To "abide" means to make yourself at home. Abiding implies staying a while. So many Christians want to see Jesus on Sunday, then check back with Him next week. Those who learn to abide can connect with God on a continual basis. Abiding means walking with Him on a moment-by-moment basis.

As you pray for your wife today, pray that she looks to Christ for all her strength. Ask God to remind her that she can't do anything outside of the power of Christ that freely flows within her. Pray that she will "make herself at home" with God throughout her day.

Sample Prayer

Father, help (*insert wife's name*) rest in You today. Remind her that the source of her strength is You. Help her remember that the Christian life is not about performance but a relationship with You. I pray she makes herself at home with You and allows You to fill her completely. Remind her today that the only way to please You is to allow Your Spirit free reign in her life.

In Jesus' name, amen.

Text Message

(*Insert wife's name*), today I am praying that you abide in Christ. I am praying that you look to Christ for strength, wisdom, and peace. The only way you can please God is by allowing His Holy Spirit free reign in your life. Today, I pray you walk with God on a moment-by-moment basis.

DAY 26

Embrace the Season

For everything, there is a season, and a time for every matter under heaven.

Ecclesiastes 3:1 (ESV)

Just as there are seasons in the year, so there are also seasons in our lives. Some seasons are for planting, others are for harvesting, and others are for rest and growth. When we fight against the season God has placed us in, it creates stress, guilt, and frustration.

For example, a mother with a newborn baby is in a special season in her life. That little baby will take up 90% of her time and energy. Empty nesters, however, live in a completely different season.

With every season comes different opportunities. When we learn to recognize the season we are in and welcome it, we can find renewed strength and fulfillment.

When we fight against the season, we often feel frustrated and helpless.

If you are in a season of building, then build. If you are in a season of caregiving, then give attention to the person who needs your care and don't feel guilty about the other things that have to be set aside.

So many times, we try and live in all seasons at once. You can't plant, water, grow, and harvest all at the same time. Your wife will find new peace and enjoyment by discovering the season God has her in and embracing it. She can enjoy each of God's seasons, understanding that a new season will soon come along.

As you pray for your wife, pray she recognizes and welcomes the season she is in. Ask the Lord to give her insight about how she can take full advantage of the season she is in. Pray that she relaxes and enjoys this time, knowing that tomorrow, a new season may begin.

Sample Prayer
Father, I pray that (*insert wife's name*) will enjoy the season You have her in right now. I pray she will recognize where she is, what You have for her today, and that she will embrace this time in her life. I pray that she will see this season as a special gift from You and will embrace

everything it offers. Help her enjoy this season, knowing that tomorrow, the season may change.

In Jesus' name, amen.

Text Message

(*Insert wife's name*), God places us in different seasons at different times in our lives. Some seasons are frantic, busy, and take everything we have to persevere. Other seasons are relaxed and allow us to rest and grow. I am praying that you recognize and embrace the season God has you in today. I pray that you celebrate the season God has placed you in. I love you, (*insert your name*).

He is Her Strong Tower

The name of the LORD is a strong tower; the right-eous run into it and is safe.

Proverbs 18:10

There are times when it feels like the enemy is on your heels and closing fast. There are times when defeat seems inevitable, and you grow weary in the fight. During those times, we all need a place of refuge and shelter.

Sometimes, your wife just needs a safe place of rest from the stress and struggles of life. During these times, she can run to the Lord as her strong tower. She can find safety, protection, and rest in Him. God has promised to be her refuge.

He is her strong tower. In ancient times, a strong tower was a place of protection. When the enemy attacked, the people could run to the tower and take refuge in the king's protection. The tower was a symbol of the king's power and presence.

God is your wife's strong tower. He is her place of safety and protection from the enemy who tries to destroy her. Too many times, we run away from God during times of difficulty. But God has lowered the drawbridge and is ready to welcome us to His place of refuge. He invites your wife to run to Him in her time of trouble.

As you pray for your wife today, pray that she sees the Lord as her strong tower. Pray that during her times of struggle and stress, she will run to the Lord. He is ready and waiting to refresh, restore, and renew her. Ask the Lord Jesus to remind her that He is her place of refuge and rest.

Sample Prayer

I pray that (*insert wife's name*) will see You as her strong tower. I pray that when she feels like she just can't make it, she looks to You for protection, provision, and a secure resting place. Remind her today that You are her all she needs. Thank You for being her strong tower. Help her to run to You today.

In Jesus' name, amen.

Text Message

(*Insert wife's name*), I am praying Proverbs 18:10 for you today. God is your strong tower. When you feel surrounded by the enemy, run to Him. If you need a place of security and rest, run to the strong tower of the Lord. He will welcome you in.

Let Her Delight in You

Delight yourself in the LORD, and He will give you the desires of your heart.

Psalm 37:4

God's desire is for your wife to delight in Him. When she delights in Him, He will give her the desires of her heart. Your wife delights in the Lord by placing complete trust in Him. She can trust and rest in Him, knowing that He is a good God and that He rewards those who seek Him. She can delight in Him because she knows He is working for her good.

God doesn't give her the selfish, sinful desires of her heart. As she learns to delight in Him, her desires become His desires. She can ask what she wants because He is molding her desires. As she learns to delight in Him, she will find incredible peace.

As you pray for your wife today, pray she places her complete trust in the Lord. Pray that she completely submits her life to the Lord. As she delights in Him, God will give her the desires of her heart. Her desires are going to line up with God's will as she learns to delight in the Lord.

Sample Prayer

Father, I pray that (*insert wife's name*) will delight in You. I pray that she will completely trust You for everything she needs. As she goes through her day, make Your desires her desires. I pray that her focus will be on finding joy in You. Help her welcome Your presence the way she welcomes her best friend. I pray she will delight in You and You will give her the desires of her heart.

In Jesus' name, amen.

Text Message

(*Insert wife's name*), today, I am praying that you delight in the Lord. I am praying you trust Him with all that you are. I know as your desires become His desires, He will give you all you desire.

DAY 29
She Can Do All Things Through Christ

I can do all things through Him who strengthens me.
Philippians 4:13

The Apostle Paul went through tremendous persecution as he preached the Gospel. He was beaten, stoned, shipwrecked, and spent months in jail. Paul preached the gospel with a literal price on his head. Most of us would have given up and let someone else do it. However, Paul was able to continue, not by his own force of will but through the power of Christ.

We all face times when we think we just can't make it. Today, your wife might experience challenges and problems, and she might feel completely overwhelmed. However, Christ is there to strengthen her. As she learns to draw on the power of Christ, she can face her greatest challenges with confidence. He will strengthen her, and through Him, she can do anything.

Today, pray your wife draws upon Christ's strength and power to face the struggles and challenges of her day. Pray that she won't rely on her own strength but on the Lord's.

Sample Prayer

Father, I pray that (*insert wife's name*) will not live by her strength alone but will draw upon the power of Christ that dwells within her. I claim this promise for her, that she can do all things through Christ. As she faces the problems and challenges of the day, I pray that You will strengthen her. I pray that she will rely completely on You. Help her to do all things by Your strength today. In Jesus' name, amen.

Text Message

(*Insert wife's name*), today, I am praying the promise of Philippians 4:13 for you. You can do all things through Christ, who is your strength. I am praying you won't try tackling the problems and challenges of today with your own power, but will instead allow Christ to be your strength.

Keep Her Alert to Spiritual Attack

Be of sober spirit, be on the alert. Your adversary, the devil, prowls around like a roaring lion, seeking someone to devour.

1 Peter 5:8

It's scary to think that Satan is out to destroy your wife, but it is a reality. One reason you need to pray for your wife every day is that she is under spiritual attack. Every day, Satan and the kingdom of darkness plots to try and bring her down.

Peter encourages us to be always watching and never to let our guards down. The verse says, "Wake Up! Pay Attention! Satan might be right around the corner, waiting to pounce on you!"

Pray that your wife will be ready when Satan attacks. He waits for a moment when she lets her guard down and is spiritually vulnerable. He loves to sneak up and whisper a lie into her ear. He loves to question the goodness and love of God. He loves to twist what God has said and use it for his own evil purposes.

Pray that your wife will be on guard today and all days against the attacks of Satan. Pray that she keeps her eyes open and her guard up, ready for his attack. Ask the Father to keep her ready and alert against Satan's attacks, lies, and deceit.

Sample Prayer

Father, I pray You protect (*insert wife's name*) from Satan's attacks today. Keep her on alert, with her eyes open for the attacks of Satan. Strengthen her as she goes through her day. Protect her from the lies Satan will try and whisper in her ear. Keep her heart close to You and her mind focused on Your word.

In Jesus' name, amen.

Text Message

(*Insert wife's name*), today, I am praying for our Father's protection over you against the attacks of Satan. I am asking God to keep your ears and eyes open to Satan's attacks.

DAY 31
His Grace is Enough

My grace is sufficient for you, for my power is perfected in weakness.

2 Corinthians 12:9 (ESV)

Struggles, problems, and suffering are all part of living in a fallen world. God never promised us that we would go through life immune to problems. However, He has given us an incredible promise that despite our problems, we have a God who cares. His grace is enough.

We want explanations as to why we are going through struggles. God rarely answers "why." What He offers is a promise: "My grace is enough." (2 Corinthians 12:9) It was His grace that loved us before we ever loved Him. It was His grace that went to the cross for us to make payment for our sins. God's grace is His love toward us.

Every problem, every attack, and every struggle your wife goes through today will be met with the grace of

God. That same grace that reached out in love to forgive her sins and made her His child in the first place is available in her time of deepest need.

God is supplying her every need because His grace is enough. Pray this promise over your wife today. Ask God to remind her that His grace is enough.

Sample Prayer

Father, I pray that You remind (*insert wife's name*) that Your grace is enough for her every struggle, every stress, and every problem. Assure her that the same grace that saved her will be there to supply her every need. Remind her that Your grace is enough for her every need. I pray she will rest in Your grace today.

In Jesus' name, amen.

Text Message

(*Insert wife's name*), today, I am praying that you rest in God's grace. I am praying that you remember that the same grace that brought you salvation is available as you face problems and challenges today. I know your every need is supplied because God's grace is enough.

Express My Confidence in Her

The heart of her husband trusts in her, and he will have no lack of gain.

Proverbs 31:11

It's important to not only express your love for your wife but to express your confidence in her as well. She needs to know how much you trust her and believe in her. Every wife wants to know that she is treasured, and that she is the most important person in her husband's life.

We men think that if we think it, our wives must know it. "Sure, she knows I love her. I said so at our wedding." We may have complete faith and trust in our wives, but if we never tell them, they will never know it.

Today, you are not praying for your wife, but for yourself. You are praying that you can express your confidence in your wife. You are asking God to work in you so you can express your trust in her and how she is a blessing to you. She needs your approval. She needs to know that you trust her. As you express your confidence in her, she will climb to new heights of confidence in herself.

Sample Prayer

Father, help me express my trust and confidence in (*insert wife's name*). I pray You will help me stop and tell her what a joy she is to me. I love her and have confidence in her. Help me encourage her to pursue all You have for her.

In Jesus' name, amen.

Text Message

(*Insert wife's name*), today, I am not praying for you, I'm praying for me. I am praying that I will express my confidence and trust in you. I know that far too often, I focus on the negative and forget telling you how much I appreciate you. I am praying that God works in my heart so that I can express to you more frequently how much I love and trust you.

DAY 33

An Example to Other Women

These older women must train the younger women to
love their husbands and their children, to live wisely
and be pure, to work in their homes, to do good, and
to be submissive to their husbands. Then they will
not bring shame on the word of God.

Titus 2:4-5 (NLT)

The world is in desperate need of people who live what they believe. We need godly, Christian women who are examples of the Christian life. Women who will not only love God and their family but will also teach younger women what it is like to follow Christ.

Every generation has the opportunity to influence the next generation in how to live in Christ. As a mature woman in Christ, God calls your wife to be an example to other women. No matter how old she is, there are always those younger who she can influence.

God calls your wife to be an example, not only to show the non-Christian world what it is like to follow Christ but to be an example to other Christian women.

Today as you pray for your wife, pray that she sets a positive example of a godly Christian woman. Pray she lives the Christian life before those who are younger than she is. Ask God to give her special opportunities to teach other women how to be a godly woman, a loving wife, and a committed Christian.

Sample Prayer

Father, today, I pray that (*insert wife's name*) will be an example of the Christian life to the younger women around her. Give her opportunities to teach younger women what it is like to be a true follower of Christ. Let her be an example in both her words and her life.

In Jesus' name, amen.

Text Message

(*Insert wife's name*), today, I am praying that God uses you as an example of Christ to other women. I am praying that you have an opportunity to influence the lives of younger women who look up to you. I am praying that you not only live the Christian life before them but also speak into their lives.

DAY 34
She Won't Worry About Tomorrow

But seek first His kingdom and His righteousness, and all these things will be added to you. So do not worry about tomorrow; for tomorrow will care for itself. Each day has enough trouble of its own.

Matthew 6:33–34

It seems that we can always find something to worry about. We worry about our health, our money, our children, the economy, and the list goes on and on. Jesus taught that if God could take care of the lilies of the fields, he could take care of us even more. Our Heavenly Father who knows and cares about our every need.

Most of the things we worry about never happen, or if they do, we have no control over them. Worry is meditating on the unfaithfulness of God. Worry is assuming God will not care for His children.

Our first priority must be the kingdom of God. If we seek God's purposes and His righteousness, everything else will work out. If we put Christ first in all we do, He will take care of the rest.

As your wife focuses on making the kingdom of God her first priority, her fear and worry will be replaced by faith in the God who loves her.

As you pray for your wife today, pray that she doesn't allow the "what ifs" of tomorrow consume her, but places her faith and trust in Christ. Pray that she focuses on God's faithfulness. Ask God to strengthen her as she seeks the kingdom of God with all her heart.

Sample Prayer

Father, I pray that (*insert wife's name*) will seek Your kingdom and Your righteousness. Help her not to worry about the issues of tomorrow but to trust in Your goodness today. Remind her that as she seeks You, everything else will fall into place. Reminder her there is no need to worry about tomorrow because You are in control.
In Jesus' name, amen.

Text Message

(*Insert wife's name*), I am praying you that won't worry about or be fearful of tomorrow but will completely trust in God's care and provision. I know that as you seek the kingdom of God, he will provide everything you need.

DAY 35
Hunger After Righteousness

Blessed are those who hunger and thirst for right-eousness, for they shall be satisfied.

Matthew 5:6

When you're hungry, it's all you think about. Every commercial, every billboard, every fast food store calls out your name. Food fills your ever thought. When you finally do eat, the food tastes better than it has before.

Jesus promises that when we hunger after righteousness, we will be satisfied. "Righteousness" means being in good standing with God – "rightness." The only way we can live righteously is to live in unbroken fellowship with Christ.

Hungering after righteousness isn't about religion or having a holy attitude. It is not about working more or trying harder. Righteousness is the gift Christ gave us on the cross. The Bible says that God placed Christ's righteousness in us!

God is calling your wife to hunger after righteousness. The only thing that will truly satisfy her is living in the righteousness Christ has given her. In other words, living as the person Christ made her to be.

Today, as you pray for your wife, pray that she lives and revels in all that Christ has done in her. Pray that she seeks God's presence every moment of her day. Ask God to show her that true satisfaction is found in an intimate relationship with Him.

Sample Prayer

Father, help (*insert wife's name*) to hunger for You. Help her realize that You gave her righteousness when Jesus died on the cross. Let her see that You have placed "rightness" within her. Today, help her to live like the person You have made her to be. I pray she will seek no other satisfaction than what she derives from her relationship with You.

In Jesus' name, amen.

Text Message

(*Insert wife's name*), the only way to find true satisfaction is by seeking a moment-by-moment relationship with God. Jesus has already made you right with God through

His death on the cross. In Christ, you are in good standing with God. Today, I am praying that God gives you a new and powerful hunger for Him.

DAY 36
Give Her Confidence in You

For the LORD will be your confidence and will keep
your foot from being caught.

Proverbs 3:26

There are many places a person can look to find confidence, but the wise person looks to the Lord. Why can she be so confident? The Bible declares that God is watching over her to make sure she doesn't stumble or get entangled and fall.

When we understand the verse "If God is for us, who can be against us?" (Romans 8:31), we can have confidence in facing our problems. We can put our confidence in many places, but when we place our faith in Christ, He becomes the source of our assurance.

The Lord is my confidence! That is one powerful confession. Pray that your wife remembers, "If God is for her, who can be against her?" Today, ask the Father to give her a new sense of assurance and confidence as she walks in fellowship with Him.

Sample Prayer

Father, today I pray that You give (*insert wife's name*) confidence. I pray that she looks to You for strength and assurance. Help her to draw on the confidence You have promised. Let her see that You are guiding her steps and protecting her from stumbling. Protect her from any trap that might be set up against her.

In Jesus' name, amen.

Text Message

(*Insert wife's name*), God has promised you confidence. I am praying you remember God is your source of confidence. You can be confident today because God is watching out for you. He is protecting and guiding your steps, so the world won't trip you up.

Extra Credit: Today, ask if you can pray for your wife. Ask if you can pray for her out loud so she can hear you. Some will say: "This is so simple; how could it be extra credit?" For others, this will be the toughest thing you have done all week. It doesn't have to be fancy. You can even use the sample prayer.

DAY 37
Mature in Christ

So let us stop going over the basic teachings about Christ again and again. Let us go on instead and become mature in our understanding. Surely we don't need to start again with the fundamental importance of repenting from evil deeds and placing our faith in God.

Hebrews 6:1 (NLT)

So many Christians never grow up spiritually. They are happy to stay right where they are, year after year. They never grow in their faith and never move on to next level of spiritual maturity. Instead, they remain as teenagers, children, or even babes in Christ. Isn't it time that we get off the spiritual treadmill and begin growing toward maturity in Christ?

Isn't it time we left behind the basics and begin growing deeper in our understanding of and fellowship with God?

God is calling your wife to become a woman who is spiritually mature and ready to be used by Him. Today, as you pray for your wife, pray she commits herself fully to become all God has called her to be. Pray she moves past the basics and toward maturity in Christ. As she grows in her walk with God, pray that she won't get sidetracked or stuck spiritually. Pray that she commits herself to becoming a spiritually mature woman of God.

Sample Prayer
Today, I pray that (*insert wife's name*) will not be distracted or detoured by the things around her, but will press on toward maturity in Christ. I pray she will become mature in her understanding of You. I pray that she will be greatly used by You as she continues to grow in her walk with You.
In Jesus' name, amen.

Text Message
(*Insert wife's name*), today, I am praying that you continue to grow in your walk with God as you press on toward spiritual maturity in Christ. I am praying that you won't get distracted or get detoured on your journey with Christ. I am praying that God calls you to a deeper and fuller understanding of Him.

DAY 38
Love God with All Her Heart

And you shall love the Lord your God with all your heart, and with all your soul, and with all your mind, and with all your strength.

Mark 12:30

One day, the religious leaders asked Jesus which of the commandments was the greatest. He gave a simple answer: "Love God." Interestingly, He didn't say, "Serve" God. God's first call is to a love relationship. Jesus then adds, "With all your heart, soul, mind, and strength."

Jesus wasn't giving us four different aspects of love, but was simply saying that we are to love God with all that we are. Love begins in our heart, works through our minds, and shows itself in our actions.

So many Christians are willing to love God at some level but not with all they are. Jesus said that if we are going to love God, we have to love Him completely. Loving God is more than an emotion or even an action, like going to church or helping others. Loving God is placing Him at the center of all you are.

God wants your wife to love Him with all she is. He wants her love before He wants her service or worship. Today, as you pray for your wife, pray that she grows in her love relationship with Christ and that she loves Him with all her heart, soul, mind, and strength.

Sample Prayer

Father, today I pray that (*insert wife's name*) will grow in her love for You. May she love You with all her heart, all her soul, all her mind, and all her might. I pray that she makes You the center of her life. Help her to submit her mind, emotions, desires, and dreams to You. I pray that she will pursue a deep love relationship with You.
In Jesus' name, amen.

Text Message

(*Insert wife's name*), today I am praying that you continue to grow in your love for God. I'm praying He becomes the centerpiece of all you are. I pray you love Him with all your heart and with everything you are.

DAY 39

Keep Her from Temptation

And lead us not into temptation but deliver us from evil.

Matthew 6:13 (ESV)

As Jesus ends the model prayer, He asks for protection from temptation and evil. Today, your wife will face spiritual attacks and temptation. She needs God's protection throughout her day. We know that God has promised victory over sin, but today, we are praying for God to protect your wife from temptation. Every day, your wife is tempted. Satan is working in the things she sees, the things she hears, and the things she thinks.

Every sin begins with a temptation, and every temptation begins with a thought. If we deal with the temptation, we can avoid the sin. Today, ask God to be with her in the middle of the temptation.

Today, echo Jesus's prayer to keep her from temptation. Ask the Father to protect her from Satan's attack. She needs God's help to watch over her eyes, her ears, her mouth, her feet, and her hands. In everything she sees, hears, or says she needs God's protection.

Today, your wife will face temptation. Even as a follower of Christ, she will be tempted to sin. She needs God's protection and deliverance. As her husband, she needs your prayers and support today.

Sample Prayer

Father, I pray that You keep (*insert wife's name*) from temptation. I pray that throughout her day, she will be protected from the attacks of Satan. I pray that You will strengthen her. When she is tempted, help her look to You as her deliverer. I pray that today, You will keep her from evil and the Evil One.

In Jesus' name, amen.

Text Message

(*Insert wife's name*), today, I am praying that God keeps you from temptation. I am asking God to strengthen you amid the temptation and keep you from Satan's attacks. I am claiming victory over every temptation you face today, in Jesus' name.

DAY 40
A Woman of Faith

And without faith it is impossible to please God, because anyone who comes to Him must believe that He exists and that He rewards those who earnestly seek Him.

Hebrews 11:6 (NIV)

Men and women of faith fill the pages of the Bible. They were people who took God at His word and lived accordingly. God is calling your wife to be a woman of Faith. He wants to grow her little seed of faith into a giant redwood of trust and reliance on God.

If we are going to please God, we must live lives of faith. We received salvation through faith, and we live the Christian life by faith.

Faith believes that God will do what He said He would do. Faith requires action. True faith shows itself in the ways we live and the ways we look at the world around us. Faith takes the word of God and moves it into daily living.

Pray that your wife becomes a true woman of faith. Day by day, ask God to build her faith, test her faith, and grow her into a woman who walks by faith in all she does.

Sample Prayer

Father, I pray that You grow (*insert wife's name*) into a woman of Faith. Take her to a deeper level of trusting You. Test and try her until her faith is proven and strong. Let her live a life that pleasing to You by walking in Faith. Let everyone she meets see her faith and praise You.
In Jesus' name, amen.

Text Message

(*Insert wife's name*), today, I am praying that you continue growing in your faith. I am praying that God takes you to a deeper level of faith, day by day, until you are mature in Him.

DAY 41
Guard Her Heart

Guard your heart above all else, for it is the source of life.

Proverbs 4:23 (HCSB)

When you lose heart, you lose everything. God knows that everything in our life flows from our heart. That's why He encourages us to guard our hearts. We must be careful what we allow into our hearts and what we allow to stay in our hearts.

Every so often, we need a spring cleaning of the heart. Just like cleaning out a closet, we need to go through our heart and get rid of any attitude, lack of forgiveness, or bitterness that we have allowed to stay for too long.

Our eyes and ears are pathways to our hearts. We need to post guard on our eyes and ears. There are some things we just cannot allow into our hearts.

A stream where people dump garbage will soon flow with filth, disease, and pollution. The same is true when we don't control what goes into our hearts. If we allow filth, hatred, bitterness, and anger to remain in our hearts, we will soon find that those same things are flowing out of our lives.

Today, ask God to protect your wife's heart. Pray she places a guard around her heart, eyes, ears, and emotions. Pray she doesn't allow things in that pollute her heart. Ask God to purify her heart and keep it tender toward Him.

Sample Prayer

Father, today I pray that (*insert wife's name*) will guard her heart. Help her to refuse things like bitterness, resentment, and fear from entering her heart. Give her strength to resist anything that might pollute it. Purify her heart and help keep her heart completely Yours.
In Jesus' name, amen.

Text Message

(*Insert wife's name*), today, I am praying you guard your heart. I am praying for renewed strength to refuse bitterness, anger, resentment, fear, and any other attitude that would take up residence in your heart. I am praying God gives you a pure heart.

DAY 42
Fix Her Eyes
on Jesus

Fixing our eyes on Jesus, the author and perfecter of faith, who for the joy set before Him endured the cross, despising the shame, and has sat down at the right hand of the throne of God.

Hebrews 12:2

When you run a race, there is only one thing that matters: crossing the finish line. The runners give their full attention to the finish line. If they get distracted, begin worrying about how others are doing, or look into the stands, they will lose.

Life is full of distractions, but success is found only as we focus on Christ. If we take our eyes off Christ, we open ourselves to all sorts of deception.

The only way to follow Christ is to fix our attention on Him. If we are to follow Christ, we must be watching and listening to what He is saying and where He is leading. There are so many shiny objects that can grab our attention. If we don't fix our attention on Christ, we will be distracted.

Fixing our eyes implies that we put our full attention on Him. We have a single focus: the Lord Jesus.

As you pray for your wife today, pray that she places her complete attention on Christ. Pray that she follows Christ wherever He leads. Ask the Lord to help her keep her eyes on Christ and avoid the distractions that come her way.

Sample Prayer

Father, I pray that (*insert wife's name*) will keep her complete focus on You. I pray that she runs toward You as an athlete runs toward a finish line. Help her avoid all distractions that might pull her away from the goal of following You.

In Jesus' name, amen.

Text Message

(*Insert wife's name*), today, I am praying that you run toward Christ with all your heart. I am praying that you focus on Christ and never take your eyes off Him. I am asking God to help you avoid all the distractions Satan throws at you so you can completely focus on Christ.

Congratulations!

Now Keep it Going!

Congratulations, you made it!

Over the last few weeks, you have developed a habit of praying for your wife, don't stop now!

Praying For Her 365

Keep it going with Praying for Her 365 If you would like a daily prayer reminder sent to your inbox, you can subscribe to Praying for Her 365.

Praying for Her 365 uses the same daily prayer format as Praying for Your Wife, however, with Praying for Her 365 you receive the daily prayer in email format. Every day you get a reminder to pray for your wife along with the topic, scripture, and sample prayer.

Subscriptions are available on a month-to-month or annual basis.

For more information about the program, visit,
www.prayingforher.com/extend

The National Prayer Room

If you enjoyed this book, why not explore other resources available through the National Prayer Room. The National Prayer Room is dedicated to encouraging prayer and spiritual awakening. Our mission is to build marriages and churches by helping Christians develop a daily habit of effective prayer.

We believe when Christians pray, God gets involved, and when God shows up, things happen.

For more information, visit us at:
www.nationalprayerroom.com

The Daily Promise

The Daily Promise podcast is a daily devotional podcast that explores one promise from the Bible every day. Each episode lasts only 3-4 minutes, so it's a great way to kick off your day with a positive, inspiring message.

For more information, go to: www.dailypromise.com

About the Author

Billy Taylor is the Founder and President of the National Prayer Room.

Through this online ministry, his teaching and training have been used in over 183 countries. He has trained thousands of men to pray daily for their wives.

Billy has been a Senior Pastor and Worship Leader in several churches. He has a passion for spiritual renewal and helping Christians experience all God has for them. He and Tammy, his wife of more than 35 years, live in the Dallas / Fort Worth metroplex.

He hosts the daily podcast and blog "The Daily Promise" at www.dailypromise.com.

Billy is available to speak at your church or event. For scheduling information contact him at billy@nationalprayerrom.com